J-707

Terry Rowe

J-707
Copyright © 2022 by Terry Rowe

Library of Congress Control Number: 2022920300
ISBN-13: Paperback: 978-1-64749-803-0
  ePub: 978-1-64749-804-7

All rights reserved. No part of this publication may be reproduced, distributed, or transmitted in any form or by any means, including photocopying, recording, or other electronic or mechanical methods, without the prior written permission of the publisher or author, except in the case of brief quotations embodied in critical reviews and certain other noncommercial uses permitted by copyright law.

Although every precaution has been taken to verify the accuracy of the information contained herein, the author and publisher assume no responsibility for any errors or omissions. No liability is assumed for damages that may result from the use of information contained within.

Printed in the United States of America

GoToPublish LLC
1-888-337-1724
www.gotopublish.com
info@gotopublish.com

CONTENTS

Chapter I	1
Chapter II	5
Chapter III	7
Chapter IV	9
Chapter V	13
Chapter VI	15
Chapter VII	17
Chapter VIII	19
Chapter IX	23
Chapter X	25
Chapter XI	27
Chapter XII	29
Chapter XIII	31
Chapter XIV	35
Chapter XV	37
Chapter XVI	39
Chapter XVII	41
Chapter XVIII	43
Chapter XIX	49
Chapter XX	53
Chapter XXI	57
Chapter XXII	59
Chapter XXIII	61
Chapter XXIV	63
Chapter XXV	65
Chapter XXVI	67
Chapter XXVII	69
Chapter XXVIII	71
Chapter XXIX	73
Chapter XXX	77
Chapter XXXI	81
Chapter XXXII	83

CHAPTER I

"Hey kid! Are you J-707?" The question was asked by a tall, lanky, red-headed youth, about nineteen.

The other boy looked up, there was surprise and perhaps a little bewilderment in his expression. It was very unusual to speak to anyone in the streets. In fact, the smaller boy was not at all sure that it was "allowed", but "allowedness" had never bothered him before.

"Sure," he answered. "What do you want with me?"

The tall youth looked around in all directions. His movements were small and jerky as if he was afraid someone might catch him talking to this small boy with dark eyes and almost coal black hair.

"Here," and with that he shoved a small package into the hands of the little surprised boy. "This is from your mother. Guard it well. Be extremely careful how you handle it. Don't show it to anyone. Do you understand?"

"From my May-tron?" asked the boy as he searched the face of the somber youth for some clue to this unexpected, but welcomed, mystery!

"No Dummy, from your mother. Remember what I said. Keep this to yourself and be very careful with it. I really don't think that you are old enough for the responsibility, but your mother had to get rid of it. The guard-trons were beginning to suspect her of having rebel connections when she was going to the fields to work."

The word 'rebel' alerted something in the boy's mind. Was he actually standing here talking to a rebel? All anxiety left as excitement began to take over his body. He seemed to forget all about the fears of whether he was allowed to stand in the street and talk with a stranger.

"Who are you?" J-707 asked the question, but his mind was so concentrated on this youth that his mouth barely moved and his voice almost didn't make it past his lips.

"I'm Tom. You may have heard of me, T-231. Well, that's me. Don't mention that you've seen me to anyone, either."

With that, Tom was gone. It seemed as if he had disappeared like puff of smoke.

The small boy stood there with his mouth open and let his mind run wild for a few minutes. He couldn't believe his own ears and eyes. He had actually seen and heard T-231.

He mustn't let May-tron know. T-231 had been a boy in his very own compound. J-707 had been too small to remember anything about the incident, but the older boys had talked about it for the last several years.

His eyes grew gray and dreamy as he remembered the stories the older boys had recounted to him. Of course, May-tron did not know the stories were being passed around. If she had she would have punished them. She would have put them on kitchen duty, trash duty, or scrubbing the floors on their hands and knees. If it was something that was a serious infraction, the person would be sent to Ultra-Max Headquarters. There he would have been put into a class which would explain why his bad behavior was not acceptable. If the offender still did not change his ways, he would be subjected to brain wave manipulation.

He had only known one person who had ever gone there. He couldn't think of anything bad that R-735 had done. But he did question May-tron's rules and was always asking why. Suddenly

R-735 was called into May-tron's office. The next thing anyone knew, he had been loaded into a mag-car and taken away.

When he returned, R-735 was confined to his cubical. May-tron and the drudge-boy-trons were the only ones allowed to see him.

R-735's best friend had bribed one of the drudge-boys-trons to let him see his friend. He took the food tray from the drudge-tron and delivered it to the confinement cubicle. When he came back, he had terror on his face and a tale that sent chills down the spine.

It seems that his friend had a strong will and mind. When he was taken to Ultra-Max Headquarters for reprogramming, the brain reorganizer machine had to be set higher than normal to effectively rearrange the cell functions which responded to the will of the individual. Instead of erasing the bad rebellious thoughts and making R-735 a loyal learning subject, it had completely erased everything in his brain. R-735 did not know his friend, in fact, he did not know anyone or anything. He had to learn how to walk, talk, eat, and think all over again. Someday, the May-tron had told them, he might regain enough mental and physical ability to work as a drudge-tron.

The drudge-trons were boys or girls that could not or would not take their lessons seriously. Ultra-Max decided not to waste any more time or energy on someone who could not keep up with their classmates. That's what would have happened to T-231 if he had been caught.

T-231 had been a very active child-tron. He had gone through his lessons quite fast and was three years ahead of his learning schedule. But then, he had started asking questions. He especially liked to ask questions of the teach-tron in his war offensive class especially about his aptitudes towards picking and choosing everyone's life style. T-231 liked to see the war teach-tron's eyes grow small and gray. Teach-tron's mouth would draw up as his teeth clamped together. His fist would clench and the knuckles would turn white.

The teach-tron tried to explain that after the final war and destruction, it was humanity that had caused chaos for centuries with their aspirations, opinions, and appetite for power.

So, the ruling committee decided to take the human component out of government and life in general. They planned a Matrix City where everything would be based upon mathematics and probability. The leaders build a gigantic computer and placed all knowledge in the computer. It was called Ultra-Max which planned and executed every facet of the new community.

That is where T-231 learned why everyone's profession or allocation ended with the word tron. It was explained that everyone should have the same classification so everyone would be equal in the sight of society. He still kept asking questions as to why the ruling committee did not fall under these rules.

That was when he had been called to the May-tron's office twice. He was warned that if he questioned the war teach-tron's credibility again he would be sent to Ultra-Max Headquarters.

After that, T-231 had become a model student. He had learned everything he could about war and technology. Later it was discovered that he had tapped into the main computer banks at Ultra-Max Headquarters and had learned many things that were "not allowed."

In his duties in the gardens outside the main compound, T-231 had become acquainted with several questionable figures. One night, T-231 had simply disappeared from his cubicle. He simply walked out of the compound gates, climbed over the city walls and somehow got through the ion barriers and into the unknown jungle.

May-tron had summoned the guard-trons. The search for T-231 had been very extensive. Seven squadrons of guard-trons had left the safety confines of Matrix City to probe through the dense underbrush of the surrounding jungle.

The guard-trons never went into the jungle alone. They feared the vicious Leo-trons and Alligator-trons which inhabited the lush green undergrowth. One squadron found a few shreds of clothing, large spots of blood, and bits of meat scattered in a small clearing about a kilometer from the place where T-231 had disappeared.

After much discussion and study, it was concluded that T-231 had met his just reward and had been eaten by one or more of the wild Leo-trons which roamed freely in the jungle. T-231 had become a hero of the whole compound. The older boys had told the story often. And, as stories are prone to do, they grew out of proportion. T-231 became a giant who had no regards for anyone and did many miraculous things. Rumors spread that T-231 did not actually die, but had joined a band of cut throats that roamed the galaxies, preying upon innocent merchant and supply ships.

Now J-707 knew that the long-lost boy was alive and was right here in Matrix City. The excitement was almost too much for the boy-tron.

Here he had a secret that even the Major-tron did not know, and he could not tell it to anyone.

CHAPTER II

J-707 could hardly wait to get back to the compound so he could examine his new acquisition.

He had given a lot of thought as to how to get his package into the compound. There was only one gate and most of the time a guard-tron was there watching and inspecting. The guard-tron had taken lots of contraband from the free-wheeling young boy-trons. S-568 had tried to sneak in a live grasshopper, and A-432 had actually tried to sneak in a run away from another compound. He had been severely punished for that. A-432 had had to stand and watch his friend be beaten. Then he was sent to his cubicle to stay for three weeks with a pulled plug. This meant that A-432 had no power. Therefore, he had no music box, no video entertainment, no computer, and, worst of all, no lights.

A-432 had to sit, eat, bathe and clean his cubicle in total darkness.

Plug pulling was one of the favorite punishments in boy-tron compounds. The length of darkness depended upon the infraction. It could range from a few minutes to several days. Rarely did it last for a week or more as it did with A-432.

A-432 was like a different person when he came out. He was nervous and jumped every time he heard an unexpected noise. He also had difficulty focusing his eyes.

J-707 remembered the ordeals of other boy-trons and shivered. He knew that he had to enter the gate at precisely 15:03. At that time the two guard-trons would be exchanging places.

Although it was "not allowed" for guard-trons to be friendly with each other, they still had to spend time in communication with each other in order for them to give and receive the report for the day's activities.

They would both enter the guard stall together. Usually they would reappear five minutes later. Sometimes the guard-trons would talk and pass along pleasant thoughts, but this could not be counted on. J-707 stood at the corner of the compound. His eyes were on his wrist computer. He held his breath as he calculated the exact second that it would be safe for him to enter the compound. At the time indicated, he walked briskly down the fence and through the gate, looking straight ahead.

His heart was pounding so loud that he was sure the guard-trons could hear it as he went past the guard stall. His fingers clutched the box so tightly that the muscles in the whole arm ached. Beads of sweat began to form. At last the tension began to ease as he passed the guard stall and mounted the ramp which would lead him into the comb shaped structure. Just a few more steps and he would be in the door and down the tube to his own private cubicle.

CHAPTER III

Suddenly a voice rang out. "Well now, J-707, what do you have there?" It was May-tron.

"Oh, May-tron, wait till you see it. It is the most beautiful and biggest dead rat that I could pick out. Life-teach-tron said I could study and dissect it. He wants me to run a life study program on Alex."

"Here, let me show it to you." He could feel the blood draining from his face. He just hoped that May-tron would not notice.

"No thank you, J-707. Just keep that box closed," She seemed in a big hurry to get away. "When will that man ever consider the composure of the compound when assigning homework?"

"And don't forget," she said. "That computer is an Al 3-369, not an Alex. In New Earth World we do not have individual names for things. We have progressed to a high point in education. We call things by their proper technical names. And your personal computer is an Al 3-369. The new model that is being given to the younger boy-trons is called an Al 2-238. It is a simpler model."

"We find that few boy-trons need an Al 3-369. Since you seem to utilize your model more than others, you will be allowed to continue with that model. Although I am not sure that Major-tron will be too happy about your tampering with it. You need to have permission when you change the circuitry." She tried to be stern, but usually she let her would-be offenders off with half a smile and a pat on the head. It was "not allowed" to be too friendly with boy-trons.

"But May-tron," said J-707. "You know that my tampering with the circuitry is only to allow me more capabilities with my Al 3-369."

May-tron was always pleased when her teaching was heeded, thought J-707, aloud he said, "I'm sure that Major-tron would approve. When he comes for his annual visit, can I show and explain it to him?"

"Hush Boy-tron," answered May-tron. "The Major-tron is much too busy to be taught by a twelve-year old Boy-tron. When he comes for a visit, you better stand clear and keep your pattering to yourself."

"Yes, May-tron, you know best."

The old woman-tron gave J-707 another hard look and shuffled off down the tube to check on the shenanigans of her other charges.

CHAPTER IV

J-707 let out his breath. He felt weak all over. It felt like a giant hand had twisted his body like a rag. Any minute now he expected his heart to come right out through his chest.

Quickly the boy-tron covered the last few paces to his door. His feet seemed to be going into slow motion. He pushed a button and the door slid smoothly back over the runners in the floor. He darted inside and then slid sideways until he was in the coat holder.

J-707 knew that the video scan and the vox, voice activated microphones, in the living part of his cubicle would surely give his secret away. This arrangement was "necessary" to maintain safety in the compound, but J-707 knew that it was discipline and not safety that the Major-tron had in mind when he ordered the devices installed seven years ago.

The only safe place for the curious boy-tron to examine his new found treasures were out of the reach of the all seeing cameras and the all hearing electronic ear of Ultra-Max. At a very young age J-707 had realized that if he wanted some privacy from the all-knowing Ultra-Max, he would have to do something that would satisfy its surveillance programming. He knew if there was an unexplained space in the audio-video narrative to Ultra-Max, a report would be made to May-tron. She in turn would call a mechanic-tron to come and haul away Alex and install another computer in his place.

J-707 had paid very close attention to the elect-teach-tron as he told about circuits and microchips. Little by little he had gone to the central store and checked out bits of electronic components. He was allowed to check out the parts under the guise of homework experiments. But in actuality, he had hoarded himself a fine little store-house of electronic parts. He had built several projects for class inspection and made little meaningless boards that would ring a bell or turn on a light.

As soon as J-707 brought the projects back to his cubicle, he would dismantle the boards and put the parts back into his hidden storehouse. When privacy became imperative, J-707 set to work to build himself an electronic privacy. He added several new boards to Alex. The added circuitry enabled him to work on Alex as a computer without the information being fed to Ultra-Max. All the while that the boy-tron was working on his computer, or doing other things that were "not allowed", Ultra-Max was receiving a signal telling that the subject, J-707, was playing a game.

At first, J-707 had chosen games like three-dimensional chess and super-sonic scrabble, but Ultra-Max made a note on J-707's report that the boy-tron was spending entirely too much time on insignificant games.

When May-tron showed J-707 his report, it was decided that he should spend more time on war games and less time on thinking games. As soon as May-tron left, J-707 promptly turned his attention into reprogramming Alex for war games. He always thought that war games were silly and a waste of time, but if that was what Ultra-Max wanted, that what Ultra-Max got.

Beside the two-sided War games, the little boy-tron had also made several special programs and stored in Alex's memory. These programs were of him self playing different games, sleeping, or doing his duty routines.

Now in his sound-proof, light-proof, coat holder room, J-707 pushed a well-hidden red button. With the push of the button, Alex began to hum into action. It searched its memory, found just the right program and proceeded to receive information of a little boy-tron as he threw his books on the sleeper, punched a button for a snack, and generally loafed around.

While the video was playing, the real little boy-tron was safe inside his coat holder. With hands trembling with excitement he began to open his new treasure. Inside were several cylindrical cipher devices that he could operate on his computer.

It only took a few seconds to put his new device into the video portion of the computer. In that minuscule amount of time, J-707 thought of hundreds of things that it might be. His imagination ranged from a new video game to a stolen "not allowed" secret from Ultra-Max Headquarters. But, he certainly wasn't expecting what showed up on the screen. It was a special letter just for him.

The image that formed on the screen was something not quite like he had ever seen before. It looked somewhat like May-tron, but not quite as used. The hair was longer, the face not so wrinkled, and the mouth turned up into a smile.

"Hello son. I'm your mother," said the soft fragile image. It sounded a lot like May-tron, but friendlier.

CHAPTER V

There's that word, mother, again. J-707 wondered what it meant and also that new word, son. The word mother always seemed to have that little possessive word 'your' before it. He hastily turned the narrative off and requested Alex to tap into Ultra-Max's vast resources and explain the new word mother to him.

It took some time for the answer to come back to the little beloved computer. "The word mother," stated the computer, "Is an ancient word. It refers to an antiquated relationship of a child-bearer-tron to her child-tron."

Well, thought J-707, it seems to indicate that a child-tron and a child-bearer-tron have a special relationship. But that was a silly idea he thought, no one ever sees their child-bearer-tron. At least none of his friends knew their-child bearer-trons.

The only people he could remember were the three different May-trons who had looked after him. He could barely remember the first May-tron. He had stayed at the infant compound for only three years, and had only vague memories of May-tron 686.

The toddler's compound was from three to six years. May-tron 873 had been there. She had been very nice to him. He could have stayed there a year or maybe even longer, but the decision to move him into the school compound came because he had showed so much interest in math and computers.

At the school compound, J-707 had taken to his studies at a very impressive rate. His teacher-trons were surprised and pleased at his abilities and interest. The new May-tron was also pleased with his progress especially the duty routines as he took over the responsibility of cleaning his own cubicle.

Once J-707 had asked his May-tron why she had chosen her job. "I took a test like everyone does and this was the position that was chosen for me. Someday you too will be tested. You probably will be a math-teach-tron or even maybe a Ultra-Max programmer," she told the little boy-tron.

J-707 was surprised that jobs were chosen for each person, but he accepted it. Everyone else seemed to accept it, however, there was a funny feeling in his stomach whenever he thought about it.

The little black-headed boy-tron shook himself out of his dreaminess into the past and turned back to his treasure. He stayed up until the wee hours of the morning. There were too many new words and ideas which he had to inquire about.

The one word which seemed to confuse Ultra-Max was "love". Ultra-Max searched its memories for two hours before it sputtered out a brief description, a few more sputters, and then it began to beep, "Not allowed. Not allowed. Not allowed."

As he listened and watched his videos, he realized that there was another type of life out there away from the protection of the compound. He was not sure that he wanted to know about this new life. Well, he reasoned, it won't hurt at least to know about it. He set his jaw and was as determined as ever that this new bit of information would not change his life or being. Still, as he listened on, there was an uneasiness in his mind. He had doubts as to the "allowedness" of these electronic books.

The ciphers told about the rebel band. The lad was so confused. According to the social-teach-tron, the rebels were murders, cut throats and thieves. The older boys had told some really hair raising, eye-popping stories about them. But this picture and the young friendly looking image just didn't fit with that type of views of the rebels that was presented in the life class.

Finally, J-707 put his newfound ciphers away in his secret place and went to bed. He had much to dream about.

CHAPTER VI

At six o'clock in the morning, the door swung open, and there with hands on hips, stood Major-tron and May-tron.

"Get up boy!" bellowed the Major-tron. "Where did you get these subversive ideas of yours?"

"Subversive ideas, Sir? What do you mean?" His heart felt like it was racing away and his hands were on the verge of trembling.

"Why did you ask Ultra-Max about the words love, mother, parents, and family? Where did you hear such words?"

"I heard them down at the museum. There was a group of people there yesterday. They were discussing ancient history. I didn't know what they meant. So, when I came back to the compound, I asked Al... Al 3-369 to please search and tell me the meanings."

He hoped that they did not notice that his face was drained of all blood, and that his heart must have been poking out through the front of his chest.

"You had better be telling me the truth, boy," said the Major-tron, his voice at a more normal level. "If I find you have lied, you will be severely punished. From now on, if you need to know more words, go to the computer in the Math-Central building. It will give you the official version of anything you need to know."

J-707 just shook his head yes and mumbled a very faint "Yes, Sir." He was too scared to answer more.

Major-tron turned and walked out, disclaiming to May-tron how he had warned the museum people time and time again not to talk about such things in the presence of such young impressionable child-trons.

CHAPTER VII

J-707 didn't know what had possessed him to tell such a thing, but it seemed right at the time. It was hard for a boy his age to understand what he had done wrong. He was a very sensitive boy-tron, and had always tried to do the right things. He had never been in any serious trouble. Even when he had tampered with Alex, it was not out of defiance or rebellion. The only reason he had programmed Alex to give himself privacy was to satisfy his own curiosity. He wanted to know things. The silly war game and childish lessons just didn't interest him. Alex was programmed to play both sides of the games and lessons, therefore, freeing himself to study, inquire, and experiment on his own.

It was still not too late, thought the boy-tron. He could still go to May-tron and explain about the crystal devices, and explain that he was too scared to tell the Major-tron about them. He was sure that with complete honesty he would get off with a light punishment. May-tron expected some secrecy from her little charges, and therefore, was very lenient if the boy-tron owned up to his mischievousness when it became serious.

But, in the back of his mind, that word "mother" kept prodding him. He had never felt that way about a word before. And, if he turned all these things in, what would happen to the Mother-tron and to T-231?

Maybe, he thought, he should just take the things down to the waste-disposal room and throw them into the dragon mouth and then everything would be gone and no one would know anything about it. But, he thought, everything would be gone.

No, J-707 knew that he could not give up the images. He also knew that this decision would shape the rest of his life. If he kept the tapes and was found out, it could mean several very unpleasant things.

He could be kicked out of elite education and assigned menial work such as food raising, waste disposal, or even galaxy patrol, a very lonely and sometimes short life. He might even be sent to Ultra-Max Headquarters for retraining.

Shivers went up his spine as he remembered R-735. Even after the completion of the retraining, R-735 was not allowed back into the elite education. He was finally assigned to a waste disposal unit on a food farm which was located in the middle of the jungle. R-735 probably didn't mind, in fact he didn't seem to mind anything. He just moved around mechanically, doing whatever he was told to do.

J-707, didn't know how, but he knew that life would now be different and if they were ever discovered, he shivered, it would be over.

CHAPTER VIII

Daily now, J-707 would select a portion of the new tapes to study. They had been made over a long period of time.

The narrator, the person who called herself, Mother, was not quite like any of the women-trons he had seen before. She seemed to be different. The smile on her face seemed very expressive. Her eyes were different, too. They were dark like his, but they seemed to do a little dance as she talked to him.

The program contained many new words which J-707 did not understand. But, he had to be very careful when he looked them up. He did not want another visit from Major-tron. J-707 would carefully make a mental list of all the words he was unsure about. He knew that if a written list was found on him or found in any of his possessions, it would mean discovery of the truth. Each day J-707 would trudge off to the learning center for his lessons. Before or after the formal lessons, he would find an unoccupied computer in one of the teach-tron's offices. He would sneak in, raise Ultra-Max and proceed to call for his information.

It was a little risky. He had almost been caught twice. He had even had to hide under the desk once. J-707 had tried the computer at the Math Central building, but explanations of the words did not fit the context of the program. Besides, the teach-trons had more computer clearance than the general public. They could ask Ultra-Max many things without arousing suspicions.

Even with the additional clearance, J-707 sometimes received a "not allowed" on his request. Things became a little easier when J-707 discovered that in studying ancient literature, he could check out a twentieth century dictionary manuscript.

Actually, he was not supposed to check it out long enough to read it, but only long enough to get acquainted with the laborious task of manually looking up words like ancient man.

As soon as J-707 saw the assignment, he knew the potential of the ancient books. He quickly faked sickness, ran towards the health cubicle, it was presumed, to throw up.

Once out of sight, J-707 darted into an, empty office cubicle. There it was not too hard to find the necessary equipment to make a copy of the needed crystal videos.

Before reentering the study area, J-707 wet his face and pinched his cheeks hard enough almost to bring tears to his eyes. One look at his damp, red and white face gave the teach-tron no doubt that the boy-tron must be deathly sick. He insisted that the boy-tron go straight to the compound and go to bed.

Once back at the compound, the boy-torn again dived into his new acquisition, stopping occasionally to find the meaning of some of the words. Hour after hour, J-707 listened and watched fascinated as Mother-tron told her tale.

The first part of the story was about a small group of people called a family unit. The mother-narrator told about one such unit. The basic unit started with a male-tron called a father and a female-tron called a mother. Then child-trons were added.

The mother narrator used the word love many times in this story. A strong affectionate feeling towards another, the dictionary had said. J-707 had once had a strong feeling toward another boy-tron. He wanted to punch him in the face. But this must mean another type feeling, because the mother-tron did not indicate that this strong feeling was bad.

As the story went on, two boy-trons were added to these units. The first boy-tron to go to the infant unit, was called, Tom, and later, Jimmy.

At this point in the story, the mother narrator looked as if she would cry. Since it was "not allowed" to have boy-trons in a family unit--he couldn't under-stand why she was crying. He was taken to an infant compound not long after he were born. Tom had gone on to one of the older boy-tron's compound.

The mother narrator went on to explain that it had been planned for the mother and father-trons to stay close to the compounds to visit and teach the boy-trons as much as possible. The plan worked fairly well for a while, but later it was determined that it was more efficient to have the boy-trons taught by one person so they would not learn things that were "not allowed".

CHAPTER IX

When he was an older teenager, T-231 was slipped out of the compound and back to the family unit. The younger boy-tron's compounds became more restricted and contact was lost. The mother narrator seemed very sad about this boy-tron being lost from the family unit.

This just didn't make sense to J-707. None of the boy-trons that he knew had even heard about a family unit. The dictionary had said that a family was a group of related people living together.

CHAPTER X

After the story about the family unit, the bulk of the story was about an ancient group of people. In the old world everyone lived in family units. Family units lived in towns and towns were grouped into different governments and countries.

J-707 laboriously had to look up all these words in the dictionary, but his curiosity would not let him give up.

It was hard to understand this older form of government. He did not know of any type of government other than his own. In his social studies, other types of governments had been mentioned, but not really explained. The governments were reported to have been so bad that they were not worth taking class time to discuss. The only government discussed in the classes was the present government and how great it was for meeting the needs of the society.

J-707 returned to the governments of the chronicles. It seemed that war broke out among the different groups. Neutron bombs ripped through the country sides. Most insect, animal, and bird life died. The oceans boiled. The fish that didn't die carried radiation poison. Sparse groups of humans could be found. Half a dozen had been spared when they took refuge in mountain caves. A few others survived when they had shared the rat's domain' in some of the remote sections of the sewers.

Somehow little pockets of civilization managed to stay alive during the time following the destruction. The whole face of the earth changed. The radioactive clouds and dust caused an extra layer in the atmosphere. This layer caused a giant greenhouse effect. Of course, the areas which were directly hit by the neutron bombs and several hundred miles around, remained like deserts, but the areas least affected by the radiation began to blossom into jungles.

It took several years for the human inhabitants to begin finding each other and organizing. There was much usable equipment still around. Some places had been remote enough when the bombs hit, only the living things were destroyed.

After a period of time, and with some extreme care, after decontamination some of the equipment and buildings could be used again. It became evident that brain power was lacking in the ranks of the survivors. There were people who were smart enough, but only a few had high technical knowledge.

As the people of the earth began to organize, these few technically educated people became the teachers, and in turn the leaders, to save man power hours, computers, that were still in working order, were put into service to help society find better and more efficient ways of doing things.

For an example a person could come to the computer center, fill in all his qualifications and interests and the computer would bring forth a necessary job that he could probably do well.

In the beginning of the New Earth this system worked very well. Many projects for the continuation of the community were completed. But, as the teachers began to grow older, they began to fear that the New Earth would not survive without them.

The leaders began to build bigger and better computers. They programmed them with every bit of knowledge they could find. The New Earth founders wanted the computers to be able to answer any questions that could possibly be raised.

The narrator on the crystal became somewhat emotional at this point in the narration. The mother-tron's video body began to tremble as she talked about how the system had expanded rule by computer and restricted the free access to knowledge for the past 300 years. The sad whimsical figure concluded that this type of system had stripped the individual person of his freedom to choose and, of his personal identity.

"Pure treason", said J-707. Then he quickly looked around to see if anyone had heard him. How he wished he had turned the contraband over to May-tron when he had first found them, but now it was too late. If the recordings were found now, he would be indicted for treason.

What was he going to do?

CHAPTER XI

J-707 didn't have to wonder what he would do for long. Certain events left no question as to his destiny. The hapless curiosity of a Maid-tron almost led to his demise. In her prying, spying way, she found the small red button which activated Alex.

She pushed it and nothing happened, so she went away. Ultra-Max began receiving a two-sided war game. When the action did not stop, the May-tron was automatically notified that one of her small charges must have skipped education classes and stayed in his cubicle to play war games.

With this information in hand, May-tron pranced down the tube to the offending cubicle only to find it empty. Upon questioning the May-tron, and examining the red button, by Major-tron a thorough search was ordered.

The crystals were found.

CHAPTER XII

J-707 had stayed a little longer to talk to one of the teach-trons. He had to kill a little time because he wanted to reach the guard gate at exactly 15:03. Ever since he had finished the mother narrator crystals he had a burning desire to know what the world was like before the great destruction, and at every opportunity, J-707 had copied ancient books.

Today he had acquired a fine copy of several ancient books. They were in several different languages, but he was sure that Alex could interpret them.

With the recorded books safely inside his clothing, the little boy-tron took leave of his teach-tron.

The teach-tron's communicator had begun to sound just as J-707 walked out the door. Little did he know that the communicator was barking orders into the teach-tron's ear to detain the little boy-tron at once.

On the way to the compound, he stopped a while in the park to sniff the smell-wells. He was not really supposed to do that, even if it did make him a little dizzy, he could see no harm done to either him or the pink and purple smell-wells.

The smell wells were metal sculpture with a long tube which was filled with a pleasant odor. The smell wells were one of the few things in Matrix city that was very colorful. They were flared at the top with different designs. J-707 became curious about the unique shapes and colors. He stayed one day after his lesions and snuck into the teacher's "not allowed" computer room to look up the word smell wells. In an ancient volume he found not only, a definition of the smell wells, but also pictures of the original specimens that were models for the sculptures.

The specimens were called flowers. J-707 had heard about flowers from some of the farm Worker-trons. The workers were "not allowed" to discuss such things, but sometimes they couldn't help showing off that they had knowledge that none of the boy-trons possessed.

The boy-trons had been forbidden to sniff the smell wells. They were told that the colorful objects were for the Worker-trons only. In the morning, before boarding the mag-bus on the way to the vegetable fields, the Worker-trons would sit on the boarding dock. There the sweet odor would flow over the crowd. It was said that the mist helped them to relax and to tolerate the long hard hours in the garden fields.

Even if it did make him a little dizzy, J-707 could not understand why it was "not allowed" for everyone except the field Worker-trons to inhaled the odors.

As he emerged from the park, a squadron of Guard-trons nearly ran over him. If he had taken two more steps, he would have been clearly in their path. As they lumbered on, J-707 wondered what desperate criminal they could be after. Rarely did one see a whole squadron of Guard-trons.

It was almost time for J-707 to enter the gates. He waited and checked his time piece. He slipped through the unguarded gate, paused a second to listen. He had heard many things of interest by listening at the gate, not that he really was eaves-dropping, but he had to make sure how long he had to get out of sight before the Guard-trons finished.

CHAPTER XIII

Suddenly, he froze as he heard his own name mentioned.
"And keep a sharp look out for boy-tron, J-707," he heard one of them say. "When you get him, send word to the Major-General-tron immediately. They found..."

J-707 did not wait to hear the rest of it. He tried to run out the gate, but each time he took a step, it felt as if a hundred pounds of lead had been strapped to each leg. Fear swept his entire body. He felt like he was going to black out, but he couldn't, he mustn't!

Although it had really been only five minutes, it seemed like an hour before he reached the gate, and another hour before he reached the end of the wall. As he rounded the corner, he thought he heard something. He looked back at the gate to see if the Guard-trons had seen him.

Wham! Pain went all-over his body and everything seemed to be going black. At first, he thought he might have hit the brick wall but as he began to fall to the ground, he realized that the object he had hit was a person, not a wall.

Fear spurred him into life. He felt a scream trying to escape from his throat, but before it could reach an audible pitch a hand was slapped over the gaping mouth. The wild eyed and thrashing J-707 looked more like a captured Animal-tron than a human.

"Quiet! Quit fighting! The guards will hear us," The voice was soft and next to his ear. It had a calming effect on the boy-tron. He hesitated a minute to look for the source of the whisper.

"What are you doing here?" croaked the now more subdued, small body.

"Looking for you," replied T-231. "We heard that you had been discovered. Mother was afraid that they would kill you or turn you into a zombie. She sent me here to get you. Just as I came up, I saw you going inside the gate. I waited out of sight then you came flying around the corner and plowed right into me."

"I thought you were a Guard-tron, and that you had me," whispered J-707.

All the while, Tom was gently leading him down a rough path which ran along the back part of the compound. Frequently he would stop and listen, then proceed slowly through the brush which was becoming increasingly thick. In the distance behind them a noise of broken branches suddenly began to rip at their clothes.

"Hurry," said Tom. "The squadron is coming. We must reach the outer area of Matrix City before they catch up to us."

"Why the outer edge of Matrix City?" asked J-707. "I would rather they not catch up to us at all!"

"We can get off the path and lose them now," said Tom, "But, if we reach the city shield without them seeing us, then we have a chance of making them believe that you escaped outside the permeable shield. That will give us several more hours. They must get permission to go beyond the barriers. That will give us time to get to our hiding place."

The shield was now in sight. It looked like the side of a giant clear glass salad bowl turned upside down. Sparks would momentarily fly through the area as an unfortunate insect incinerated itself by trying to fly through the nearly invisible shield. There were no animals in Matrix City but bugs and insects had managed to get in.

"Wait here," cautioned Tom. The tall lanky boy-tron hurried toward the shield. Two strides took him dangerously close to it.

Suddenly, Tom pushed a button on his bracelet and jumped through the shield. J-707 blinked as Tom did this. He had only seen one other demonstration of the anti-magnetic wrist generator. The bracelet, produced an anti-magnetic shield around the individual and allowed the person to pass through the protective shield which surrounded the city.

The smaller boy-tron watched in wonder. It was still very dangerous, he thought. If the person going through the shield tripped or touched the ground before he was completely through the barrier, then there would be a short display of fireworks and the person would be as charred as the hundreds of unfortunate insects which tried daily to pass through the electronic curtain.

Tom leaned over a bush and caught a piece of material on a thorn. With this done, he again pushed the button and sprang back through the shield.

"Why did you leave that piece of material out there, T-23?" asked the boy tron.

"My name is Tom. You will get used to it sooner or later. I put that material out there because it is a piece of your dirty clothing that we took from your cubicle several months ago. We thought it might come in handy," Tom told him.

"Why did you take a dirty suit and where is the rest of it?" asked the terrified little boy.

"You ask too many questions," replied Tom. "We took a dirty suit, so someone would think you had been wearing it, and the rest of it is out there in the jungle, covered with your blood, locks of your hair, and microscopic bits of your skin, and before you ask, we collected these things when you went for your yearly health exam. The Nurse-tron is one of us." The story seemed very familiar to the small black eyed boy-tron.

"That's the same pattern that was followed when you disappeared, T-2, I mean Tom. Won't they get suspicious?"

"No," said Tom. "They take all the evidence to the lab and analyze it. Feed the information to Ultra-Max and it comes up with the answer: 'eaten by Leo-trons'. It is programmed to act only on the information at hand. Similar cases are not studied. And, if someone does get suspicious, all he can get from Ultra-Max is the statistics of deaths in a certain period of time."

CHAPTER XIV

It was getting dark now, Tom was pushing J-707 into ever much smaller places. Finally, Tom pushed him under a tree branch. It felt like he was only a foot from the forest floor. The branches made a dwarf tunnel.

The tall lanky Tom seemed to be having less trouble walking bent over in the prickly tunnel than the shorter J-707. Tom was quick and sure-footed. As they pushed their way through, the branches seemed to close in behind them.

Outside eyes would probably never guess that two human-trans had ever walked that way. The brush was thickening. J-707 thought that surely, he could go no farther, but he did. Every time he would pause, Tom pushed him from behind. The branches and needles tore at his skin and clothing.

Just as he thought he would become a bloody mess, he tripped and landed on a, not too smooth, rock. He got up and started to push on, but Tom beckoned him back to the rock. The branches had cleared a little here and both Boy-trons could nearly stand up.

Tom tugged and strained at the rock. J-707 wondered why the older Boy-tron was trying to move the heavy object, but he was too tired to ask, and too bruised to help. Little by little the rock began to move, but it began to move upward instead of across the ground, as J-707 had supposed it would have moved.

"Quick," called Tom. "Put a stick or something under the edge."

J-707 forgot how tired and bruised and bloody he was, and snapped to attention. He hurriedly looked around and found several sticks, but he discarded four of them before choosing one he thought would support the rock.

As he placed the stick beneath the rock, he realized that this was no ordinary rock. In fact, it was not a rock at all, but a steel plate decorated with a huge heavy rock.

When the stick was safely in place, Tom released his hold. The stick wavered, it looked as if it would break, but finally settled into place.

Tom lay on the ground with his sides heaving. "Now what do we do?" asked J-707. It took a while for Tom to regain his breath.

Still gasping Tom said, "We wait. When we opened the door, it sounded an alarm. Someone will come soon."

Suddenly, a large Rat-tron appeared in the opening. It seemed to grin at the Boy-trons and then scurry away.

"Oh," said J-707. He was ready to run in the opposite direction.

"Don't get frightened," said Tom. "That is our signal that someone is there."

Tom leaned over the small opening under the rock. He hit the rock three times and spoke softly into the opening. "This is Tom. We are being pursued."

As soon as the last word was muttered, a rumbling and squeaking sound became very audible. The rock and steel plate began to move upward. Soon it stood perpendicular; to the ground exposing a circular opening about twenty-four inches in diameter.

"I'll go first," said Tom. "You follow me fast as you can."

Tom began to disappear into the hole, apparently climbing down a ladder.

As soon as Tom's head was below the surface, J-707 started looking for a way to get down into the hole. It was a long tube-like chamber with steps cut into the side.

J-707 began to climb down, his head had barely cleared the opening when the heavy rock lid started its descent.

The light began to dim, and J-707 found himself in total darkness, darker than he had ever been in. Matrix City always had light. Icy fear swept over him again for the second time that day.

"Don't be afraid," called Tom from somewhere below him. "You can't go anywhere but down."

That thought was not very comforting to the small boy. He could feel the circular walls touching him on all sides. The thought of that grinning Rat-tron kept running through his mind.

It felt like hours before he reached the bottom of the tube. And, to his surprise, Tom was not there. Fear again began to take over. Suddenly a small noise caught his attention. He was afraid to move.

CHAPTER XV

"Come on," It was Tom again. "Find the opening and come on in." J-707 began to feel the circular walls. He then found that one section of the small tube had backed away which left a space large enough to walk through.

Groping through the opening, the tired small boy found a small passage way leading into another chamber. He heard the door closing behind him. At the same time, a door opened in front of him, flooding the area with welcomed light.

J-707 stumbled into the lighted chamber. It took several seconds for his eyes to become used to the light again. Slowly different figures began to emerge into his sight.

There was Tom. His back was to the boy-tron and he was talking to several men-trons who were hanging on his every word, as he recounted his day's adventures.

Before J-707's vision was completely recovered, a pair of hands came out of the darkness, grabbed him, surrounded him, and squeezed him so tightly that he could hardly breathe. He thought he had been kidnapped and brought here to be killed.

Finally, he was able to fight clear of the smothering hug enough to see who was squeezing him. It was mother narrator. J-707 wondered what he had done that was so terrible, that she was trying to squeeze him to death. At the same time, her face did not look as if she was mad at him. But she must be, he thought. She was crying. He had seen very few humans cry. Only small boy-trons. And, that was only until they learned that crying was "not allowed."

"Jimmy, we are so glad to have you back at last," said one of the voices from the darkness. J-707 looked all around to see to whom the voice was referring.

Then he slowly realized that he was the missing boy-tron, Jimmy.

CHAPTER XVI

J-707 had a million questions, but they would have to wait. As soon as the greetings were over, the group made preparations to leave. The mother-narrator must have known how tired and sore he was, because she saw that he was lifted onto a large long object call a bed along with Tom. With blankets and heavy covering around them, it was not long before J-707 fell asleep.

CHAPTER XVII

The next morning, after two hours of wandering through the dimly lighted watery tubes, the group emerged into a clearing. It was dark with only the lights in the heavens, which he had not seen before, to illuminate the darkness.

J-707 jerked alert and looked toward a large glow in the distance.

"That's Matrix City," said Tom.

The boy-tron's heart jumped. He now knew what he had feared. They were in the middle of the dread jungle. Tom saw the pale scared face and tried to calm Jim down. He told him that most of the stories that he had heard about the jungle were just rumors, some were started because the farm workers had seen something and were afraid to go to work that day. He also said that some of the stories were told by the family groups to help keep people out of the jungle. If you were careful and kept alert nothing would hurt you.

After several more hours through the sometimes dense jungle, they found the group inside a small primitive looking compound. The fence was made of wood and pointed trees instead of steel and stone, but it still looked like a compound.

Jim, as everyone called him, was pulled off the beast which was he had been riding, called a horse. He was then hustled into a rough mud and log building. It had been a long day since this morning—or at least he thought it was morning. It started when everyone got up, dressing, eating what was called a breakfast and then prepared to leave the big room with the animal shaped beds and the round wooden tables.

At the end of the day he was tired. He had walked around watching people, and even shyly, talking to them. He had decided that these people were not going to hurt him. He helped pull up things called weeds until he was replaced by a girl-tron who said that he was pulling vegetables too—whatever that was.

After what was called the evening meal he was glad to climb into a bunk. He was asleep before the mother-narrator could cross the cubicle and turn out the lights.

CHAPTER XVIII

A strange warm light awoke J-707 the next morning, or rather the next mid-morning. Later he was to learn that this new phenomenon was sunlight. Of course, he knew about sunlight, but in Matrix City, there was no sunlight. The protective shield filtered out most of the sun. Huge mercury, sulfur, and zinc lights illuminated the city twenty-four hours a day. The brightness was just about as great, but the lights were cold, not like this warm friendly sunlight.

J-707 rubbed his eyes. He got out of bed, and tried to push it back into the wall like the ones at the compound, but couldn't. He gave up and wondered what they did with beds in the daytime.

With hunger, pains grew in his stomach, and he went through the door in search of someone and some food. They didn't seem to have the replicator, like in Matrix City. There you could go and get food almost anytime you wanted it. Of course, you were given a daily allowance and couldn't go over it, but you could save up in case you wanted a special item.

This group seem to have just three eating times called breakfast, lunch and evening meal. They also had what they called snacks. These were dried fruits, nuts, and oatmeal—things he had never heard about.

The next room was a little noisy. There were four human-trons sitting around a little hollow cube with a solid top. He was later to learn it was called a table. It took up a lot of room, not at all like the retractable food trays like the ones in his compound. The people sat around this table instead of standing like everyone in Matrix city. Not only did they sit, but they sat together and talked to each other. It was allowed here to relax when you had to ingest food, and you could even sit and intake food more than five minutes at a time. Things were so different. The food was so different. He had to watch what the others did, before he could eat. They used things called forks. The food in Matrix City came from a machine. You pushed a button and out came a nourishment bar. J-707 had to admit that the soft, squashy food on the flat circle tasted better than the dry bars.

In Matrix City, eating had not been important: it just met a daily requirement. Whenever a person was hungry, he simply went to the dispenser, took several of the well-balanced squares, and ate them, and went on about his business.

The morning meal, there are no vendors here, consisted of two round "eggs", two white circles with a smaller yellow circle in the middle, and two pieces of flat brown squares things, a substance called honey, and a glass or two of the white juice called milk. Jimmy didn't know that his old food had tasted so badly until now.

Mealtime was the one thing that Jimmy grew to like better at the rebel compound than at Matrix City. It was not just a necessity, but was a real treat to rest and visit with each other.

"Mother-narrator," said J-707, one morning at breakfast, "Why are things so different here than in Matrix City?"

"Just call me Mother, Jimmy," answered the slender young woman.

"Matrix City was built upon the laws of mathematics," butted in Tom.

"Yes," said Mother, "Everything was streamlined for efficiency."

"No one has to make decisions," said Tom. "They are all made for you." You are told what to eat, what to wear, and what your occupation will be."

"The worse thing about the government, is that families are told when and if they can have children. And then the children are taken away and are not cared for by the family anymore," said Mother.

"But, if these things are so bad, why do they happen?" asked Jimmy.

"After the destruction, many of these things were necessary," answered Mother. "There were too many people and not enough food. If children had been born at the wrong time, it might have meant, not only starvation for the babies, but also for the parents and others."

For several hours, Mother talked about the history of the New Earth. It was just like listening to the crystal stories, except now Jimmy could ask questions when he didn't understand something.

Right after the big destruction, no children were allowed to be born. But, as the earth began to grow more food, it became apparent that younger people were going to be necessary to replace the older ones.

Food was still a factor. The leaders did not want a lot of non-productive people being brought into the world to share the food and not the work. If a couple wanted children, their characteristics and health histories were fed into the computer. The computer would analyze the data, and describe what type children would most likely be born to that couple. Based upon the data, the computer would either accept or reject the application.

During the rebuilding time, many parents had to work long and hard hours. Some of the older adults, who could no longer be productive at manual labor, would take care of the young children. As time went on children had no family life at all. They were raised by strangers. Eventually, not only were couples told if and when they could have children but even their mates were chosen for them electronically.

It was a belief that people of the New Earth would be more productive if they were not allowed to choose to be creative. Artists, musicians, and poets were no longer necessary. Only scientists, mathematicians, warriors, and workers were considered important.

There was a group of artisans the computer did pick—whether they had any interest or talent. These people were to design the cities, houses, and things like the smell wells and pleasure parks. Jimmy had never heard of pleasure parks and asked what they were.

It was explained that pleasure parks were designed for citizens that were not able to join the work force. It included mentally slow, physically disabled, older workers who had reached the age of 70, and injured workers. The injured workers were hopefully there until they recuperated and could be returned to their occupation.

"That's the government's ideal of being beneficent," sneered Tom.

"What's wrong with that?" asked Jimmy. "It sounds like a good idea that the government takes care of people that can't do things for themselves."

"It sounds great," answered Tom. "Did you ever buy or work for your own food?"

Jimmy shook his head no. "We were given tokens that we placed in vending machines." He went on to explain that if they were not prudent and used their tokens up too quickly, they went without food and drink the rest of the month, unless a friend shared his allotment with you.

"Did you get to pick out your own clothes, or decorate your room, or choose the subjects you wanted to study?" Tom continued to ask.

After three hundred years of this type of training, people were little better than twenty-first century robots. Hence the suffix tron was applied to everything. Living things merely became extensions, and an actual part, of the ultimate computer. Every part supposedly equal to every other part. If that was true, thought Jimmy, why did Major-trons seem to have more power than the May-trons or Guard-trons?

That was the exact question that got Tom into so much trouble when he had been a student. The type of life that Jimmy heard being described did not seem bad. It was all that he had known. He would probably go back to the boy-tron compound right now if it was not for the fear of being retrained at Ultra-Max Headquarters. Maybe, he continued to hope, if he told them all about the rebels, they would be lenient on him, but he could not really take the chance. The Major-tron might not listen to him or might not even believe him if he did listen.

Another thing that Jimmy thought about if he ever got back to Matrix City would he be expected to tell on these people who had protected him? He was so confused. He did not want to see these new acquaintances get into trouble. He did not know what it meant to have a friend because that was "not allowed", but there was a feeling toward these new people that he had never encountered before. Tom and the others had actually risked their lives to help him.

Maybe having a friend meant that you, not only cared about what happened to another person because it might happen to you, but that you tried to help that person get out of his difficulties.

There was that other word "trust" that the rebels were always using. Jimmy had heard that word used many times. The last time he had heard it was when May-tron and Major-tron had told one of the boy-trons to "trust them that he would not get into any trouble if he told them about what M-577 was doing." It was true, the boy-tron did not get into trouble, but M-577 disappeared. It was rumored--when boy-trons found a place to talk without being overheard by other people-trons or electronic-trons--that maybe M-577 had been put out of the city into the food plants. There he would work in the grow food plots, process the food into the nutrition squares packaging them for vending machines, and generally working for the food service of the city. He would not be able--or would he want to--go to outside the food compound because of the ferocious Lion-trons and other Animal-trons.

Maybe the word trust meant to gather information on others who were doing "not allowed" things and turn them into authorities. Jimmy's feelings were all confused. All his training had told him that rebels were bad, yet he could not go back. Like it or not, he was a rebel.

Six other people lived in the compound. Jimmy asked one woman if she was also called mother.

"Yes," she answered, "But not by you. My own child calls me mother. You are to call me Aunt Ruth because I am your mother's sister."

"And, you call me Grandmother," said an older woman with white hair. "I am your mother's mother and your aunt's mother." The tone of her voice seemed to indicate that her statement should explain things, but it didn't. At least, family relationships did not become clear to Jimmy right away

Another inhabitant of the compound was Jimmy's cousin, Luann. She was bright for a girl-tron, but she seemed to have a very superior attitude. Not like any of the other girl-trons he had ever seen. Of, course most of the girl-trons he had seen before were in the maid and working crew.

Girl-trons that were accepted into the elite education program went to another compound on the other side of Matrix City. Jimmy wondered if the girl-trons in the education program were as superior acting as this new-found cousin.

Aunt Ruth's mate was called Hudson, whom Jimmy was to call Uncle Hudson.

Uncle Hudson would get up early and leave the compound. Sometimes he would be gone all day. Jimmy learned that Uncle Hudson went into the jungle to tend to the food. He would take the small herd of goats and cattle to a small fenced in area. Then he would work in another fenced area which was called a garden which was known as the grow food region.

Sometimes he would go into the jungle to gather edible plants. Here, he had to be very careful. Many of the plants which, before the destruction, were good and tasty had changed to bitter and foul-tasting things. Some were even poisonous. Some people, who had survived the destruction, died because of choosing and eating malignant plants. Even after three hundred years, the plants could still be poisonous. Jimmy later learned there was a team of the rebels trying to breed the plants to get rid of the defective poisonous genes.

At Matrix City, people did not have to worry about poisonous plants. The cook-trons used only nutrition squares sent in from the farm cities. At the farm cities, plants were raised in hydro-trays. They did not need soil. Each tray contained the minerals and water that the plants needed. Huge lights automatically turned on and off to give each type plant the exact light needed. Each batch of plants was tested and certified as safe. A small amount of seeds was saved for the next year's planting. The remainder was ground into an edible, but tasteless, paste be made into squares and shipped to the cities.

The farm cities were located well outside the city walls. Jimmy had visited a farm city on a field trip one day. Since it was forbidden to travel in the jungle, Jimmy's class had to travel on a mag-car bus. These were magnetic cars which were able to reverse magnetic polarity with varying degrees. This enabled the driver to use the magnetic force of the earth to propel the car upward or to be drawn downward by the earth's force field.

It took several years to learn to drive a mag-car. One small wrong move and the car would be dashed to the earth with such velocity that only splinters would be found, or propelled upward with such a tremendous G-force that the occupants would be killed. Jimmy thought that someday he would like to be able to drive one of these magnificent cars or maybe even a spaceship, but that was before he realized that people did not get to choose what they wanted to do. Now, what could he do? He was an outcast, a rebel. What lay ahead of him now that he was away from the city, away from the computers, and out in this primitive compound.

CHAPTER XIX

Since Jimmy was smart, he had always been treated rather special. He had never before worked hard with his muscles. His teachers all had great hopes for him. He probably would have been the head of Ultra-Max programming someday.

Now in the rebel compound, Jimmy worked long hours. At first it was hard because his muscles had to adjust to increased activity. The first few days he went with Uncle Hudson to work in the garden. That had been exhausting.

Jimmy had been awakened before day light. It was hard to get used to the idea that one did not have light all the time as in Matrix City. Of course, when Jimmy had wanted to sleep, all he had to do was to simply turn off his light and go to bed in his light tight room. But the rest of the city was filled with brightness. Many people carried on their business whenever they felt like it. Student life had been more regulated so that everyone would be sleeping about the same time. But here, in this new experience, life was regulated by the great ball of light called the sun. When it came into view and even sometimes before people got up. Of course, some people like guards and maintenance workers, worked in the dark time and slept in the light time.

It was still early morning when Jimmy and Uncle Hudson left with the goats and three scrawny head of cattle. "I know we drink the white juice from the goats, Uncle Hudson, but what good are these cow-trons?" Jimmy asked.

Uncle Hudson explained that someday they would have a herd large enough that people would be able to eat meat again. The only time they ate meat now was when someone killed a wild animal in the jungle, or when they had enough rabbits or chickens to kill a few. But, there was not enough cows around to eat beef very often.

In fact, there were not too many animals in the jungle. Most had been killed in the destruction, but small groups were beginning to flourish again. Some of the larger animals like the Leo-trons, lions, had not only flourished, but had multiplied to such a degree that they had become a menace to other forms of life. This was one reason that the rebels had been allowed to live unmolested in the jungle compounds miles away from the protected cities. The inhabitants of the city were too afraid to venture out into the forest.

Several years after the destruction a count had been made of the various animals around the cities. These figures had been entered into the computer and multiplied by the total area of the land. In reality this gave a greatly exaggerated number especially with the Leo-trons. The large beast had been drawn to the city by the smell of fresh meat.

With the faulty data, and the fact that humans were usually attacked when they left the cities, orders had been issued from Ultra-Max that no citizen of the city was to venture outside the walls alone, and then only if ordered to do so on official business. This made it easy for the rebels to leave the cities, manufacture their own death scene, and never be bothered again.

The officials of the cities knew there were people living in the jungle, but the official ruling from Ultra-Max was that, because of the Leo-trons, no one could survive for very long. Therefore, no one was to go after runaways past a certain distance from the city walls.

All of this puzzled Jimmy. He had been brought up not to question Ultra-Max, but here he was out in the middle of the dense jungle hours at a time and found none of the horrors described by Ultra-Max.

Day after day, Jimmy worked with Uncle Hudson. His small thin arms and legs begin to show small ripples of muscles. His hands were now covered with small patches of hard skin called calluses. At least now his hands did not break open and bleed when he pulled and cut weeds from the precious edible plants. Jimmy was beginning to enjoy this new life. The bitterness he had once felt was gone, but he still missed his studies and the exchange of ideas with the Teacher-trons. Most of all, he missed his beloved Alex. He knew that Alex was impersonal and inanimate, but Alex had personality. Jimmy missed trying to outsmart his elders and their sophisticated computer. In that way he was much like his older brother, Tom.

Jimmy wondered what Tom and the others did all day. When he asked, his questions were ignored or else answered vaguely. Jimmy didn't worry about it too much. He was too tired at night to do anything much except eat and go to bed.

One night, he lay very restless upon his cot. The noise in the next room woke him several times. He would close his eyes and drift back into a restless sleep. He came awake suddenly realizing he had heard his name.

"He's got to know some time," came the voice in the other room.

It sounded like Tom.

"But I just don't know if he's ready yet," came the reply. It was Uncle Hudson.

Well, thought Jimmy, maybe I am going to find out something now. Maybe I'll find out where and what Tom and the others do all day.

"Maybe you're right," said Uncle Hudson. "Soon we are going to need all the man power we have. If you think he is ready to start working out in the mine, we'll try it."

The mine, thought Jimmy. He had heard about mines before. Silver, gold, coal, and copper mines were familiar words to him, but they were a long way from Matrix. City, and they were usually worked by prisoners. Prisoners were people who had committed petty crimes like stealing food or getting drunk and laying off work too many times. They were not usually sent to Ultra-Max for retraining because they were from the working group and were not expected to produce any greatness. Therefore, they were sent to the mines for a specific amount of time. When their sentences were up, many just continued at the mines because that was the one place they could be assured of a place to live with food to eat, and not any real thinking.

The small face was lost in thought. How, he wondered, could this rebel group be connected with corrections department?

As Jimmy drifted back into a light sleep, his dreams began to take odd forms. Rocks suddenly changed into grinning faces which looked a lot like Tom and Uncle Hudson. The rocks seemed to grow arms which had whips at the end. Every time Jimmy tried to run through the hole in the rock one of the whips whirled in his direction. It was all he could do to scamper back out of the way. The very walls seemed to be crushing in on him.

Jimmy was breathing heavily with drops of sweat running across his body as a soft voice cut through the darkness and a warm hand touched his shoulder. As his eyes opened, the tense lines in his face began to relax. The smiling warm face gazing down upon him was Mother. Peace flowed through his body.

CHAPTER XX

Several days went by without any more mention of the mine. Jimmy's imagination ran wild. He just knew that Tom and the others ran a prison mine. He shivered each time he thought about chains and bracelets going around his legs and wrists.

The morning of the dread event came too soon. Jimmy got up as usual, washed his face, and was half way through breakfast, when Uncle Hudson's announcement came.

"This morning, Jimmy, you will go with Tom to the mine instead of with me," he said. His face held no particular expression of malice or anger, so Jimmy did not know how to properly react.

"What will I do in the mine?" asked Jimmy, tightening his muscles so that his voice and face would not betray the anxiety that he felt.

"Wait and see," said Tom. His face now broke into a friendly smile. "I think you will like it."

After breakfast, Uncle Hudson left for the garden as usual. Mother and Aunt Ruth began to pick up all the dishes and clear the table, Grandmother went to sit by the window and started her sewing. Luann and Tom went into their rooms to dress.

"Hurry up, Jimmy," said Tom. "We do not want to lose too much time." Tom led the way out the door and through the woods into a clearing. There, disguised as a large tree, stood a mag-car. Tom brushed aside the branches and opened the door.

"Get in," he said.

Jimmy hesitantly followed him into the steel bullet shaped contraption. "Were you trying to hide it, Tom?" asked Jimmy. He thought to himself that it wasn't disguised very well.

"Yes," answered Tom. "But not from the ground view. Patrols do not travel this far into the jungle, but they might fly over on their way to a farm city or prison mine. We didn't want to take any chances on someone seeing this one. It has been reported as wrecked by Ultra-Max so no one will be looking for it, but we, just didn't want people to get curious about why a mag-car should be out in the middle of the jungle."

The remainder of the ride was fairly quiet with only a few comments about the scenery. At last, it seemed like hours, the mag-car with its three occupants, eased down into another clearing.

Tom covered the top and sides with branches. With this done, Tom started through the woods at a brisk walk with Jimmy and Luann following. In only a few minutes they came upon a hole covered with out-reaching branches. Tom turned sideways and disappeared into the thick foliage. This reminded Jimmy of the escape route. He hoped that he wouldn't get as scratched up this time.

After passing through the branches, they entered a spacious tunnel like structure. It was hard for Jimmy's short legs and small steps to keep up with the lanky tall boy, but he managed to keep Tom in view. This doesn't look like a prison mine, thought Jimmy. Where are all the guards?

"This is another section of the ancient sewer system through which we escaped when we got you," explained Tom.

Jimmy had wondered about the other people that he had seen that night of the escape. He wondered if they were here in the mine. On that account, he was correct. Tom pushed a few buttons and a large piece of rock slide sideways revealing several people whom Jimmy did not know. But, instead of them chipping away at ore in the walls, they were seated at small tables. On each table was a small computer. Jimmy stood there with his mouth agape.

The people greeted Jimmy and were pleased to see him.

"Here you are, Jimmy", said Tom as he pushed the boy to a vacant table. "Here is where you will be working."

Jimmy could not believe his eyes. There on the small table stood a small computer. It must have been a twin of his beloved Alex.

"It looks just like Alex," he sputtered.

"It is Alex," said Tom.

"It has taken a lot of time to recircuit him so he would not transmit anything to Ultra-Max. We had to do a lot more work on him than expected. We are fairly convinced that he is safe to use now."

Jimmy had to turn away. He did not want anyone to see the tear that slipped out of the corner of his eye.

It was too good to be true. His own Alex back with him again.

CHAPTER XXI

"How did you get him?" asked Jimmy.

"It was really very easy," said Tom. "The educators were going to get rid of it long ago, but since you showed so much promise, they let you have the more advanced model. When you ran away, they didn't have anyone to use it, so they called the central supply at Ultra-Max to come get it. Well, we have a man at central supply, so he went to the compound and picked it up. Instead of taking it back to central supply, he just brought it here."

Jimmy was only half listening. He was rubbing, patting and checking all the switches on the little computer. Alex hummed alive as Jimmy turned on the power switch.

It took several weeks for Jimmy to get reacquainted with Alex. He had to adjust to him without all the extra circuitry. Tom explained that they did not want Alex to give them away if he were piped into Ultra-Max. Jimmy had to start all over again. Each time that he built a new circuit, it had to be inspected and passed by at least three of the elder workers before it was approved.

One thing that upset Jimmy was the fact that all his work was checked and rechecked, and, all of his work was just routine. Putting little problems, that he could work without a computer, into Alex and recording the results. It gave Jimmy a slow burn to know that his cousin, Luann, was working in the blue room. She did all her work by herself with very little supervision.

The blue room was top strategic work. Jimmy was not sure exactly what went on in the blue room, but he was sure if his girl-tron cousin could do it, so could he.

"She's older than you and more experienced," replied Tom to Jimmy's questioning.

"We're a team," said Tom. "We're not in competition with each other. The project is important. If you have to get ahead and compete with your cousin, or with me, then you will be removed from the project."

Removed! thought Jimmy. I just got Alex back and now he's talking about taking him away again. Jimmy turned away. He did not want anyone to see the hurt expression on his face.

"Don't worry, Jimmy," said Tom, in a much softer tone. "We all started in the general formula room. It is a training room. When the elders are convinced that you know basic programming in several programming languages, then you will be moved to the blue room."

"In the blue room you will be given a problem," continued Tom. "The problem will be a segment of a much more complex program of Ultra-Max. The object will be to modify that segment."

Jimmy felt a little better. There were many things to which he had to adjust. At Matrix City, girl-trons and boy-trons were educated differently. He had never seen a woman as a teacher-tron. The only type of computer he had seen a woman using was a fixed computer used for ordering supplies and things like that. It usually had a few buttons that were used for ordering, retrieving information, bookkeeping and other mundane work. He had always been under the impression that females and the worker groups were mentally inferior, and now, he was having to rethink his whole short life.

CHAPTER XXII

After three months, Jimmy was allowed into the blue room. He replaced Luann. She had now been sent to the red room.

In the blue room, programs were made and tested. In the red room, they were fed into the computer link which would feed information into Ultra-Max. One wrong move and Ultra-Max would know someone was tampering with its programs and might even be able to reverse the link and find them or even sabotage the organization.

Some programs were accepted by Ultra-Max, but most were rejected. If the team in the red room could not modify the program enough to get Ultra-Max to accept it, then the program was sent back to the blue room for a rewrite.

In Jimmy's first problem he was to design a program to deal with the older people. Jimmy was quite shocked when he ran the Ultra-Max program and found that the older people were not in existence. At least he didn't know where to find them. He knew that he had never seen very many elderly people before, but it never occurred to him to ask what happened to them. It took him several days to find where they were hiding.

At age sixty, the people were relieved of their positions. Then they were taken to a retirement compound. There they stayed until they died. Each was given a job either of housekeeping, cooking, yard work, or caring for the infirmed. They were not given a choice, but were given whatever position was available at the time.

Another three weeks of searching through the archives before he found the rationale for this procedure. "Why should we change things?" asked Jimmy. "It looks like things are going well."

Tom explained why things had to change.

Three hundred years ago, because of hardships, life expectancy was only in the late forties and early fifties. But, every person was important and had to help the colony to survive as long as possible.

In the early days, if a person made it to age sixty it was considered an honor, and if possible, they were given a reward for their long hard work by giving them a place to live in beauty and peace for the short remainder of their lives. But now, people live to be seventy and eighty and more. Because Ultra-Max was not programmed to change with new paramours the older citizens were locked into an uneventful life sentence for twenty and sometimes thirty years.

"Many died early," said another of the elder men. "Some go crazy. Their lives are now useless. We must do something for these wasted humans."

The hard part was not writing the program, but writing it in such a way as to get Ultra-Max to accept it. Ultra-Max is self-analyzing and self-mending.

"You are the third person to work on this project, Jimmy," said Tom. "We need to find a way to make this program work."

"How many things have you changed in Ultra-Max?" asked Jimmy.

"Not too many," said Tom. "We usually don't get a complete change, only bits and pieces."

"Why not try to get to Ultra-Max and change him physically?" questioned Jimmy.

"We have a man on the inside right now," said Tom. "In a few months he may be in a position to do just that, but right now he can't get close enough to touch it."

The days drifted into months. Still Jimmy could only make minor changes in the elderly program.

"Don't get too frustrated," said Tom. "We work on it for a while and make as many changes as we can and then we let it set for a while. I like the way you have confused the date selection. If Ultra-Max keeps skipping the selection dates the law will still be inefficient, but no one will be called to retire. That will slow things down for a while."

Jimmy didn't let it show, but his pride was nearly bursting right out through his skin. He had finally done something that pleased Tom. He was finally going to be accepted and not treated like a child.

CHAPTER XXIII

Most mornings, Tom, Jimmy, and Luann were usually met with smiles and greetings. This morning was different. The mag-car was met at the landing by two grim faced team members.

"They've got him! They've got Michael," said John, the taller of the two.

"Someone recognized him. They have him in an old abandoned security cell. They searched through the computer banks to see what to do with someone who is back from the dead. When they couldn't find anything, they decided to execute him like an ancient criminal. Michael asked them to search the banks for the rights of the criminal. There is a little-known law which entitles the accused criminal to be heard before a panel of judges." This was explained by the two worried men.

"He has one chance to convince the judges that he is not a criminal and should not be executed for treason. There has not been an execution in over two hundred years. When the law and life, was computerized, it left very few avenues open for capital offences. And, all other petty 'crimes were taken care of in the penal mine, or wherever the computer decided to send them."

Jimmy and Luann tried to keep up with the conversation, but it was hard to understand all that was happening.

"Who's Michael?" asked Jimmy.

"He's my uncle and your father," said Luann. "I thought you knew."

Jimmy did not really grasp the significance of having a father. He had not seen him. All that Jimmy knew about fathers was the relationship he had observed with Uncle Hudson, Aunt Ruth and Luann. He knew that there was a special bond between them.

Even though he did not know Michael, his father, by the way everyone was talking, he knew that there must be something special in this man.

Program activity ceased for the next few days as the rebels tried to regroup and plan future strategies. "What are we to do without our leader," exclaimed some of the underlings.

"We were just beginning to make progress breaking Ultra-Max codes, now all is lost."

"No!" shouted Tom. "If we let our work stop then all of Dad's work and death will be for nothing."

"He's not dead yet, Tom," choked his mother as the tears began to flow down her face.

"It's just a matter of time, Mother. We all know the risk when we started this project."

"No! Tom," said Uncle Hudson, finally. "We are not going to let my brother die without a fight."

From then on, the group seemed to unanimously acknowledge Hudson as their new leader. Tom, Uncle Hudson and several other of the leaders were in endless conferences.

Jimmy, Luann, and other lesser computer workers were put on hold as far as the Ultra-Max programming was concerned. Now their time was spent in searching the archives, especially those concerning the laws that were established since the great destruction, for some type of legal help.

CHAPTER XXIV

Michael's defense was to be simple and direct. He was to simply state and explain the law as the early fathers had viewed it. He was to try to explain how the many little laws and rules became a tangled web which snared the people into slavery.

Most of the government leaders were reasonable men. The rebels felt sure that at least their side would be heard. They felt that a compromise could be reached. The rebels were even willing to offer an agreement to refrain from tampering with Ultra-Max's programming in return for the freedom of their leader and freedom to live their own lives.

The sacrifice could mean complete separation from Matrix City. It could mean that the many years of work could come to a grinding halt. The steering group decided that the promise of non-interference would not be offered until all else had failed. They felt the city elders could not pass up the opportunity to get rid of the rebel influence forever or at least for a generation or two.

On this point of the defense, Michael was not consulted. He had already stated that the work to humanize Ultra-Max must go on under any circumstances.

CHAPTER XXV

The room chosen for the trial was a large gothic type room with plush chairs behind a long slim table. There was one short backed chair with a little less padding then the others. This one was for the prisoner.

There were exactly ten, twenty-foot, unadorned benches with straight backs for the gallery for the on lookers. There would be a pre-selected' number of spectators. Most of them would be from the ruling echelon.

The trial would not be open for the general public, but would be televised through all computer systems. Anyone, including the rebels, could watch the trial. There was a special communications line set up in case anyone had some special evidence to be included. All they had to do was to punch a button and then type the information into their own computer. The Ultra-Max special branch would take the information and decide if it was important. If it was relevant to the case, the main branch would be informed and then passed on to the judges.

The rebels had already cracked the code to get patched into the main information bank. They knew they could interrupt anytime to offer them a deal.

CHAPTER XXVI

The small crowded office contained three men. An unarmed guard-tron stood just out of hearing in the hall. Two men in flowing loose fitting robe sat, one behind the desk and the other to the side, both looking intently toward the standing man. Michael stood there, looking taller than usual, dark eyes nearly piercing through the two seated men.

"So, you see, Michael, that A-7003, D-473, and myself, B-805, decided that we were incompetent to decide such important matters ourselves. Therefore, we have put Ultra-Max in voice transmission. He will be voice activated and he will hear your case." The balding robed man sat beaming at Michael.

"No!" shouted Michael. "You can't do this! Ultra-Max is not a he! It is a machine. An unfeeling, unthinking, mechanically logical thing."

"Oh, we will hear you, Michael, but we must have help with such a great decision," assured the smaller, soft spoken man.

At this point on, the trial went from bad to worse. Every time Michael made a statement about Ultra-Max or about the realism of computer imprisonment, Ultra-Max would groan and moan. The circuit from the hearing room to the household computer would be shut off and only the people in the immediate room could hear the appeals for a better life.

If it had not been for B-736, a lesser dignitary, a rebel himself, who was able to secure a place in the gallery, then the rebels would not have known any of the proceedings.

CHAPTER XXVII

Luann and Jimmy listened intensely as the computers sputtered and wheezed. Ultra-Max had, undoubtedly, had not been programmed for defense. Nothing could be said which would even be a hint of imperfection in society.

Some of the rebel computers were finally reprogrammed to override the weak audio shut off from Ultra-Max, but the video could not be resumed.

The hopes that Michael would get a fair unbiased hearing was now replaced with the feeling of hopelessness. Doom and gloom hung over the rebel stronghold as all ears strained to hear the squawk, crackle, and distorted speech as Michael tried to appeal to the humanity of the judges.

The days droned on. The gloom became heavier and heavier. The ultimate offer of complete inactivity of the rebel band was not made. Uncle Hudson and the others felt that Ultra-Max was incapable of making such a decision.

Several times the judges would ask questions of Michael trying to expand a point or two in his story, only to be met by the wailing voice of Ultra-Max.

"No need to question the traitor, I have already digested the information," It belched.

Michael complained about the use of the word traitor. It was explained to him that Ultra-Max's vocabulary was limited and since he was being tried for treason, Ultra-Max just put a label on the defendant.

Michael reluctantly acknowledged the explanation, but in his own mind, he knew that Ultra-Max had already convicted him.

CHAPTER XXVIII

"I can't stand much more of this," choked Luann, as she began to cry softly.

"Maybe we can do something," whispered Jimmy. "Meet me outside in ten minutes."

With those words, Jimmy quietly withdrew to the shadows and then through the door to the outside. No one noticed him leave. And no one noticed ten minutes later when this action was duplicated as Luann withdrew from the solemn room.

Outside felt better. The sun was shining with a cool breeze floating through the trees. There was no hint of death there.

Luann found Jimmy sitting on a ledge, overlooking a green peaceful valley staring out into space.

She just stood there, afraid to shout, afraid he might be startled and fall. Soon he looked up and noticed her standing there.

"How long have you been there?" he asked.

"Not long. What were you thinking so hard about?"

"We, I mean I, can disrupt Ultra-Max."

"That's silly," answered Luann. "You see what happened to Uncle Michael when he tried to tamper with Ultra-Max. What makes you think you can succeed when Uncle Michael failed?" Her words tumbled out hoping that what she was saying wasn't true, and that maybe this small clumsy kid did know some way to help.

"I know my way around Ultra-Max Headquarters," he answered. "Remember, I had a class 8 clearance. I could go anywhere in the building I wanted. I was supposed to have an adult with me, but many times I would sneak out at sleep time, enter my card into the electronic locks and spend several hours studying Ultra-Max. If the locks haven't been changed, I can still get into the building."

"And," said Luann, "If the locks have been changed, it will set off an alarm and then what, father and son trials?"

"That's a chance I've got to take," said Jimmy. "At least I have to try."

"You'd better change that back to we," said Luann. "I'm going, too."

Try as he may, Jimmy tried to resist this last request, but Luann was determined. He would have to take her since she threatened to tell the others if he left her there.

In a way, Jimmy was glad. Two people can summon more technical data than one.

CHAPTER XXIX

Getting into the city was more of a problem than getting into the Ultra-Max complex. Jimmy and Luann had borrowed the magcar and driver. They told the driver that they were to go to the old merchant ship dock just outside the city. They explained that they were running an errand for Uncle Hudson. The driver was to come back for them in three hours.

The old dock was still in use. The old rebuilt spaceships were used to travel from one pocket of civilization to another. Not only could cargo be transported to and from the different cities but also to the farm cities and back.

Luann had brought a pocket full of mother's sweet rations, she called candy. This had always been an effective way to bribe the working people. With promises of four more of the precious candy pieces, a crew member agreed to take them both into the city gates. They were passed off as two peasant children entering the city to work.

Jimmy had brought along his cadet uniform. He had to mend and enlarge it in several places. He had borrowed a matching pair of pants from Uncle Hudson and had altered them. He looked like a cadet from a distance, but he could not afford a close inspection.

Luann had brought a peasant maid uniform. The rebels had learned long ago that a maid or maintenance uniform could get them almost anywhere.

Jimmy's student card still worked. He and Luann passed through the main doors. It was a good thing that the card alone would open the great gates and heavy doors. Some places required a voice or fingerprint identification.

The Ultra-Max compound was sparsely inhabited as Jimmy and Luann arrived. Everyone was watching the trial on their own private computer. Even the working class was given special hours so they could watch the trial proceedings. Each time Ultra-Max disconnected the proceedings the working class would receive, not the static and distortion, but entertainment type programs. Their computers were preset for entertainment instead of education. The working group was always the working group. They could never change from one station in life to another once they had been so classified.

Luann preceded down the halls about ten meters ahead of Jimmy. In her maid's uniform she could encounter any of the Guard-trons and give Jimmy a chance to hide. The Guard-trons were less likely to become suspicious of her than of him. They would probably think that it was just another dumb peasant who wondered into the wrong building.

All the precautions were needless, because there were very few people in the building and those who were, had their minds on the trial. Finally, a huge massive iron door loomed into sight. Ordinarily, this was a voice activated door, but since there was a lot of activity at certain periods of the day, it was left open during the peak work hours.

Luann and Jimmy looked up and down the halls. Finding no one around, they ducked inside the dimly lit morgue like room. It took a few minutes for their eyes to adjust to the diminished light.

From this room, three other doors led into other places.

"We go through the middle door," said Jimmy.

Passing through the door, they found themselves in another hallway. Jimmy took the lead. He moved quickly down the hall to the final door at the end.

"Well, here we are," said Jimmy. "We are in the connection room. If we go through the left door we find the power supply unit. It should not be too hard to disconnect it from Ultra-Max."

"How long will it take for them to fix it?"

"If we knock the power supply out, it will disable Ultra-Max for quite a while."

"How long?" demanded Luann.

Jimmy's eyebrows knitted together as he calculated the time element.

"Anywhere from six to eight weeks," he answered.

"That's not enough," she said. "We must disable him for good. He had taken enough explosives from the farm compound to blow the central Ultra-Max complex to pieces."

"Yes, but--," Jimmy stammered. "That would be--almost like murder."

"You think that it is not going to be murder when Ultra-Max pronounces his verdict on Uncle Michael?" she demanded. "I know you don't know your father, but it looks like you would have some natural feelings for him. He is your own kin."

Jimmy thought a minute. "I don't know how to feel about him. As you said, I don't know him, or about fathers, but I do know mother feels very sad about him being a prisoner and that makes me sad. That's why I want to help him. But, all my training has been geared to maintaining and protecting Ultra-Max. From the time I. can remember, the greatness of Ultra-Max has been driven into me. Now, you are asking me to do something against everything I have ever believed in."

Soothingly, Luann spoke, "'You have got to use your own mind and judgment. You must decide logically if your training and brain washing is true or if your new experiences and family really mean anything. Don't become a machine!"

"I know you're right, Luann," said Jimmy. "I know what I must do. We must save Michael, if for no other reason, for Mom's sake."

With this decision firmly in mind, Jimmy became very businesslike. He became the commander.

"Give me the explosives, Luann. I want you to go to the store room where the library banks are kept. In the utility room, you will find three lines against the south wall. The middle one has a connector coupling it to the main line going to Ultra-Max. Take the wrench on the wall and undo the connector. I'll give you exactly ten minutes. You must <u>not be</u> touching anything in that room when the explosives go off. If you are not successful in ten minutes, leave it anyway. I want to save the library data banks, but not if it would mean any danger to you. Don't take any unnecessary chances."

"You either," she said softly as they synchronized their watches and went their separate ways.

Luann went back down the hall to a door they had passed earlier. Jimmy went to the door on the right. He knew where he must place the explosives in order to do the most damage. He would not set the explosives until nine and a half minutes. There were sensors on Ultra-Max which might be able to alert the security in time to prevent the demolition.

CHAPTER XXX

The third day of the trial had really taken the toll on Michael. His appearance had drastically changed. The eyes were darker and seemed to have sunk a little more into their sockets.

The trial was beginning to tell on the elders as well. They also seemed more subdued, more, gaunt in appearance, and more irritable. All these signs were bad for Michael's outlook. Everyone wanted to finish the trial, to get back to a normal life style, and to try and sweep away this rebel problem.

"Let's begin," announced A-7003. With that, he hit the gavel and everyone sat down.

B-805 stood up, faced Michael, and asked, "How long will this take, Michael? You have already given us a history lesson from three hundred years before the destruction, through the destruction, and now, to a hundred and fifty years after the destruction. When are you going to get the present time and the present problem?"

"Please, your chairmanship, I've been trying to give you an overall view of why we have the present problems. Every time I try to make a vital point, Ultra-Max interrupts me and stops my story. I've asked you to please turn it off! We'll never get anywhere this way. Use your own minds to decide my fate."

But the last words were lost to the senate hearing. Ultra-Max had countered with a loud whirling noise like that of a hurricane with crackles and flashes like lighting.

Michael, unable to out-shout the cosmetic noise, sat down, dejected.

The trial droned on, or rather screeched on, through the day.

The time for the daily adjournment was near. Suddenly, from Ultra-Max came some unearthly sounds.

"Security! Security!" shouted Ultra-Max. "Security, to the central complex, immediately. Someone is tampering with me. Hurry! Hurry! They have stuffed explosives under my main encasement, the fuse has been lit. Hurry! Hurry!"

The voice took on an eerie sound, the screen turned yellow, then green. The people were taken by surprise they could only look on and wonder what was happening.

Ultra-Max again belched out, "You may be able to destroy me, but I'll blow every computer and circuit connected to me. All of your protective shields, lights, computers, and food dispensers--I'll destroy them all. And, don't forget, Elders, I have now armed destruction II."

The climate control center began to smoke, the air became too heavy to breathe. The gallery became chaotic. People started toward the portals by twos and threes. Some people were caught in the crowd and forced forward with the crushing weight of the human avalanche.

As Michael was being swept toward the door, he turned and got a last glance of Ultra-Max's smirking screen. The look of satisfaction seemed to hang on the grotesque screen as smoke and sparks blew the terminal apart.

Outside, panic had hit the inhabitants. The people were running wildly and shouting hysterically.

Finally, Michael was able to catch up with the two elders.

"A fine thing you and your rebel band have done now Michael," shouted B-805.

A-7003 began to speak, "Yes, Michael, we were beginning to get a glimpse of your life. Now you and your kind have destroyed us. Be merciful to us and kill us now. We do not want to go through the future."

"What do you mean?" asked Michael. "I did not know about this myself, but at least now maybe we can all live in freedom."

"We will not live," said B-805.

Again, A-7003 took up the conversation. "Ultra-Max controlled everything. Our climate, our light, our food, everything!"

"Yes," said Michael. "But, all these things can be done by man. We don't need a machine to run our lives."

"Yes, Michael. We know that the rebels have been living their own lives, and can live independently of Ultra-Max, or for that matter, Matrix City, but you heard Ultra-Max say that he had armed the second doom," said the elder, looking older and graver than before.

He continued. "Our forefathers feared that war would again break out among the different groups. In order to keep eternal peace, the old unexploded nuclear bombs were wired into the central unit. One bomb for each city. You see, Ultra-Max is the central control for all the cities. Matrix City is the largest, but all the minor cities derive their power from Ultra-Max. So, when it was threatened, it armed the bombs for revenge. We have forty-eight hours until doom."

"Yes," said B-805, "We were given forty-eight hours in case of war, we would have time to reconcile. If we did, then a new key could be punched into Ultra-Max and he would then disarm the bombs."

"But now, all is lost. Ultra-Max has not only been destroyed, but he has destroyed all equipment which was connected to him as well. Even if we knew the access codes to the bombs, we don't have any computers in working order to disarm them. We don't even know if the link to the bombs is still intact," said A-7003. All the while he talked, he shook his head in defeat.

"We've got to try," said Michael. "Life is the most important thing we have. We must fight to keep it. And if we can't disarm the bombs, then we will again have to take to the sewers for refuge."

"Yes, Michael, maybe we should do things your way. What should we do first?" asked A-7003.

"First," said Michael, taking command, "We must stop the panic. Get the people under control. Don't tell them about the bombs. I'll try to take care of that. You get the people to gather food, water, and supplies, and store them in the sewers in case we fail to disarm the bombs."

"We will try, Michael, but panicking people are hard to control when their only security has just blown up in their faces." Even as he said the words, new hope seemed to radiate from A-7003's face.

CHAPTER XXXI

Luann and Jimmy had somehow managed to get back to the compound. Jimmy's arm had been hit with some flying debris, but with all the excitement, no one noticed.

Michael arrived at the mine to find confusion and total darkness. His strong commanding voice had a calming effect upon the inhabitants. Jimmy's mother pushed her way through the crown and grabbed Michael with such force that it almost choked him.

The greetings and celebrating for Michael's return was short lived. Michael, the imposing figure that he was, gained control of the situation and commandeered their attention.

"Friends and family," he said in a very stately, almost formal voice, "I need to know what happened to Ultra-Max. Who ordered it and what was done?"

A deep silence settled over the group as, one by one, the leaders in turn denied knowledge as to what had happened. Jimmy tried to speak. He was not sure if it was the awesomeness of Michael, his father, or the fear to know the consequences of his own acts, that produced the large lump in his very dry throat.

Finally, he was able to squeak out, "I did it!"

Even through the dimly lit candle light, Jimmy could see or rather feel all eyes piercing through him.

Michael looked puzzled. As the light of recognition dawned upon him he said, "You must be Jimmy. I'm your father."

With that said, Michael offered a hand to Jimmy which the boy took and was very reluctant to let go. Michael pulled Jimmy to him and hugged him tightly. "I never thought I would see you," he said.

After a minute, they both regained their composure. Then Michael spoke very softly to the boy. "Why and how did you disrupt Ultra-Max?"

"I," said Jimmy, almost in a sob, "Wanted to help. I didn't know that the power would backlash into all the support systems." Jimmy could barely hold his head up to meet Michael's eyes.

"I made him do it," sobbed Luann. "He wanted to take out the power supply and delay things, but I made him blow up the computer instead."

The room was totally silent as the words of the two young people sunk into the grim minds of the older group.

"That's treason," said someone in a very hushed tone. "We may all be punished."

Michael again took control and said, "It doesn't matter. We had planned to get the people out from under the control of that machine. It was just done differently and sooner than we had planned. The power did not backlash, Jimmy. Ultra-Max purposely destroyed all systems connected to him. We have a real problem confronting us now. We must sit down, decide what is to be done, and act quickly, or else the New Earth World is doomed forever."

Quickly, Michael finished telling the story about the bombs. He concluded, "We must divide into groups. One group will work with the people and the elders to get enough food and water stored in the sewers in case of another destruction. Another group will work on the power plants to restore the lighting and power to the city. The third group will search the ruins and try to find enough computer parts that will enable us to override the final orders of Ultra-Max. That group will also look for an electronic connection to the armaments. You can use Alex," said Jimmy. "I disconnected him from Ultra-Max before we went to the headquarters."

Luann added, "And, we disconnected the library and reference banks. We may be able to find the information we need there."

All this time Michael was appointing and grouping people and was halfway to the door when he heard a loud thud. He turned around to see his son, Jimmy, lying on the floor, blood oozing from his shoulder.

"Tom, you will take Jimmy's place with Luann and myself working with Alex," said Michael. "Your mother and Aunt Ruth will have to care for Jimmy. He looks as if he's lost quite a bit of blood."

CHAPTER XXXII

Jimmy could hear noises and see faces, but they all looked blurry and the sounds were not distinct. He kept having night mares in which giant machines with legs kept chasing him. The faster he would run, the slower he moved. Finally, a face he recognized appeared. It was his Aunt Ruth.

"Well," she said, "Are you going to wake up and join us?"

"Where am I? Where's Michael? How much longer before the bombs destruct?"

"Relax," she said. "The bombs would have blown up hours ago. You lost a lot of blood, and maybe had a concussion. You have been asleep for two days."

"You mean I missed all the fun?" he asked.

"All the fun?" the voice was that of Tom's, but Jimmy had to stretch his neck around to see him.

"We worked frantically night and day finding that code. It was a good thing you disconnected the library, we would have never found it. Even after we found the access code, we didn't know if we had interrupted it or not. We had to wait until the final second to know. When the bombs didn't go off, we knew we had interrupted things."

"What about the people of the city? What are they going to do?" asked Jimmy.

"Well," said Tom, "Uncle Hudson and his party had a time trying to convince the people to work together. One group was in the city looting and stealing. They were given their choice to either stay out in the city with their loot or come into the tunnels with the others and take orders like everyone else. The bomb and the fear of the lions finally made good citizens out of most of the thieves.

Tom continues, "By the time the bomb scare was over, Uncle Hudson had calmed the people down and talked them into forming a government. They even chose leaders. A-7003 is the ruling chairman and our father, the vice chairman. Also, teams were sent out to different cities to organize them. It will not be too difficult. They just thought they had a power outage. They didn't know Ultra-Max had been destroyed and therefore, they were not in a panic."

"That's enough," said Aunt Ruth. "Jimmy needs to rest."

Jimmy was getting tired. He wanted to leap out of bed, but his eyes started to close instead. He drifted into a deep but natural sleep.

Again, Jimmy began to dream. He was riding high in the saddle with his face feeling the wind. When he looked down, instead of the gentle horse he expected, he was astride the four "footed" giant computer which had tried to crush him in his earlier dreams and he knew now everything was going to be alright.

www.ingramcontent.com/pod-product-compliance
Lightning Source LLC
LaVergne TN
LVHW041537060526
838200LV00037B/1032